This edition published by Parragon Books Ltd in 2014 and distributed by

Parragon Inc.
440 Park Avenue South, 13th Floor
New York, NY 10016
www.parragon.com

Written by Peter Bently   Illustrated by Deborah Melmon
Edited by Laura Baker   Designed by Ailsa Cullen
Production by Richard Wheeler

ISBN 978-1-4723-1998-2

Printed in China

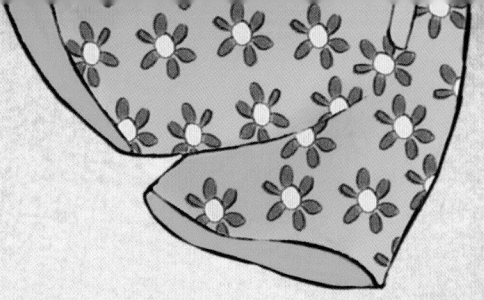

UNDERPANTS
WONDERPANTS

PaRragon

Bath • New York • Cologne • Melbourne • Delhi
Hong Kong • Shenzhen • Singapore • Amsterdam

Is it an eagle?

Is it a plane?

NO—it's **underpants wonderpants**
to the **rescue** again!

Whenever you
need him,

in **sun,**

snow,

or **shower,**

he'll **fix** all your problems with

UNDERPANTS POWER!

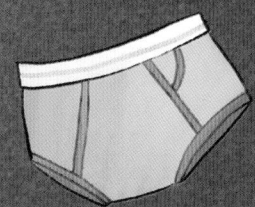

"Elephant **sat** on our nest!" **grumbles** Mouse.

"No problem!" says **wonderpants.**

ZAP!

An **underpants** house!

Polar Bear Cub
can't keep up in the **storm.**

ZAP!
Thanks to **WONDERPANTS** she's **cozy**
and **warm!**

Kangaroo cries,
"I've been **itching**
all night!"
ZAP!

In this hammock,
the insects can't **bite**!

The fisherman's ripped a **big** hole in his net. ZAP!

"**Help!**" cries the Queen.
It's so far to the ground—

WONDERPANTS'
Pantachute
helps her
land
safe and **sound!**

WONDERPANTS zooms to the river,
and in a **great swoop**—

he puts out
the **fire** with his
SUPER-PANT-SCOOP!

But that's not
the **end** of his
super-pants day ...

An **alien** spaceship is heading this way!

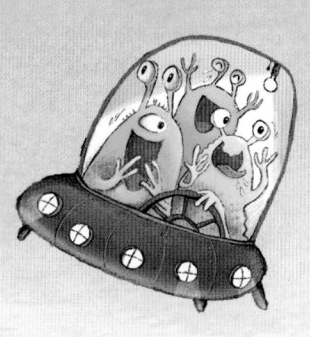

The **creatures** are

grinning and **shaking**

with **mirth:**
"As soon as we **land**

we'll take over the **Earth!**"

But **imagine** the look on
each **alien's** face

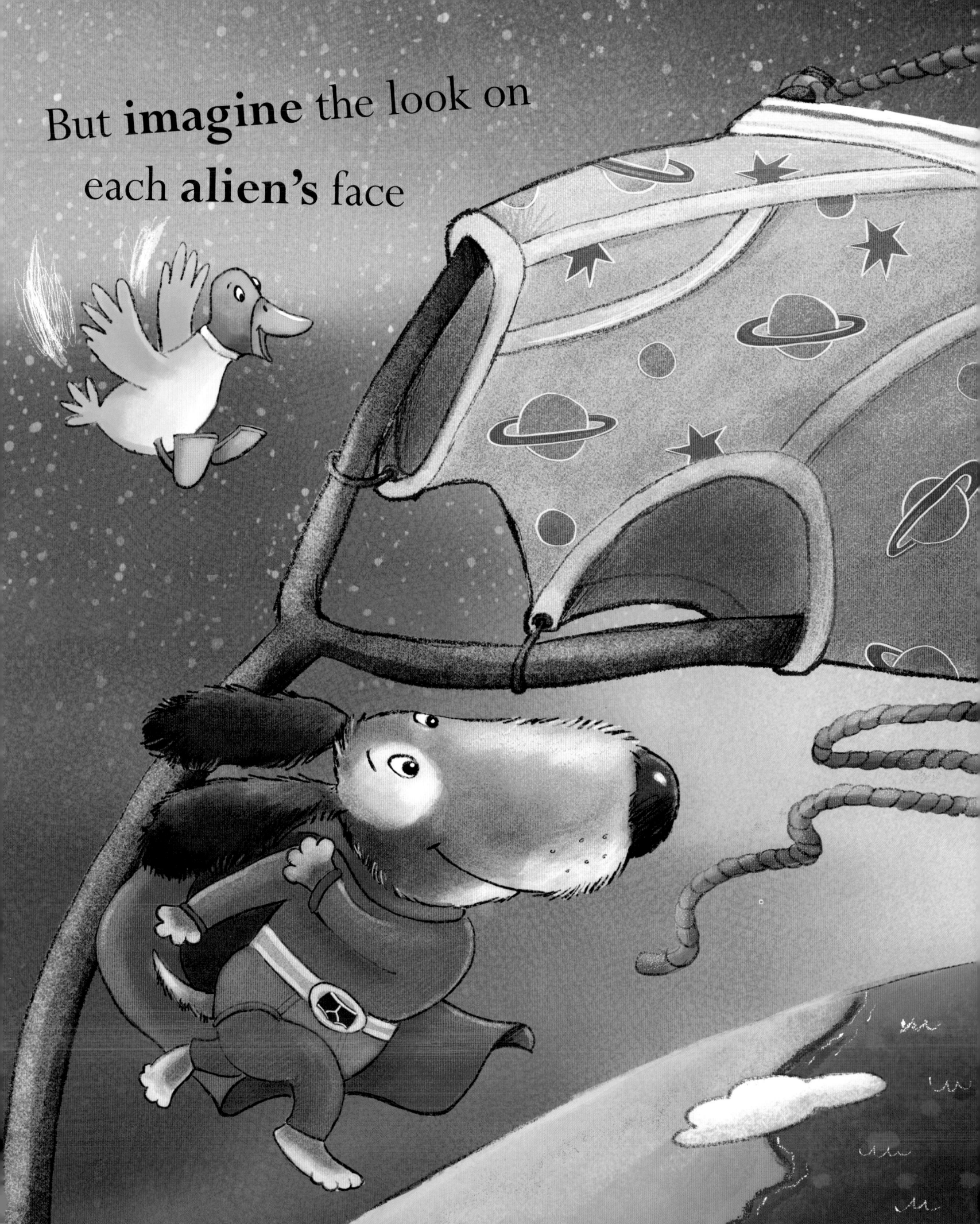

when a **WONDERPANTS**

sling sends them—**ZAP!**—back to **space!**
The people all **cheer**
as they **watch** from afar:

"**WONDERPANTS**
saved us all—

"He's our
SUPER-PANTS STAR!"